GOOD MORNING, SELF
MW00930602
Written by Jaquay Murray
Illustrated by Jessica Goes

GOOD MORNING, SELF

As a mother, I know the struggle of getting your child to wake up truly excited for each new day. It's the early years that we need to begin to teach them how important self-care is. Learning to care for their mind, body and to pour love into themselves first. With this practice, each day, children will learn to begin their day with cleansing breaths, positive thinking and physical health.

GOOD MORNING, SELF

Written
By
Jaquay Murray

Good morning Self! I'm so thankful to wake up today!

Let's begin the day in a positive way.

Before I get up out of bed I will take
3 big deep breaths deep down in my belly.

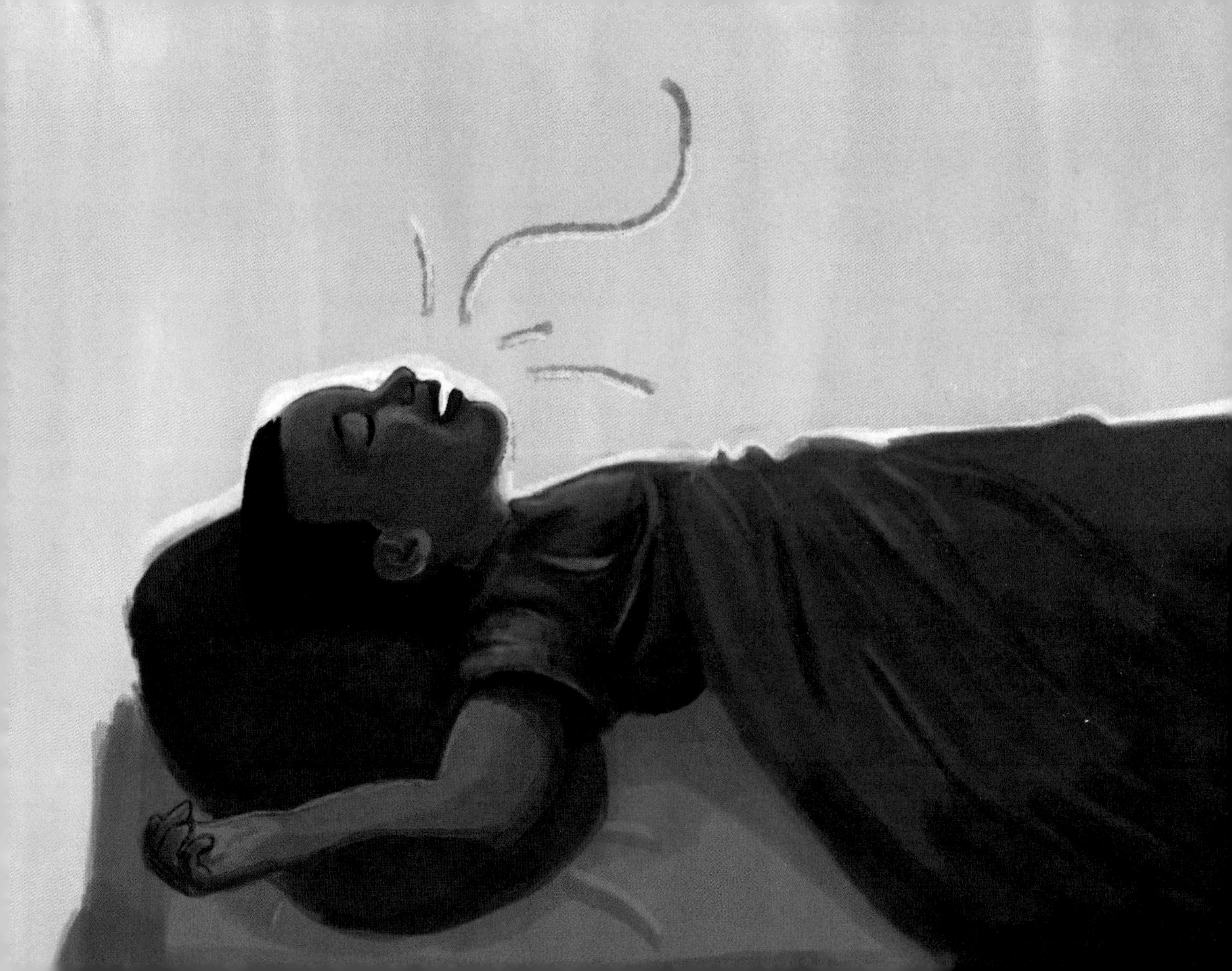

I begin waking up my body by wiggling my fingers and toes.

Now is the perfect time to think of 3 reasons to be grateful each morning.

I'm so grateful for waking up today!

I'm grateful for waking up with a fresh start
and new possibilities, like a new high score!

I'm grateful for my loving friends and family.

I'm grateful for the possibilities of tomorrow,
like riding my bike.

I jump up out of bed and start my day.

Stand with my feet apart, reach my hands up high and stretch and I say, today I want to feel energized.

Now, I stretch my arms out wide and reach wide like a starfish and say, today I want to eat a healthy meal.

Now I reach down low to my toes and say, today I will conquer something new.

With my feet in place I twist to the left at my waist and look over my right shoulder.

Then twist to the right and look over my left shoulder.

I'm waking up my body inside and out.

I end my quick morning stretch with my hands together in front of my heart.

I take 1 last deep belly breath.

I start my day in a positive way by taking care of my mind and body first.

When I care for myself I can better care for others.

GOOD
MORNING,
SELF

It is my hope that each time you read this book to your little one that you discuss what you are grateful for and develop your own morning routine. Taking time to begin each morning with cleansing breaths, stretching, moving your body and positive thinking. Building a self-care routine in the early years and planting the seed that before you can care for others you must first care for yourself.

Reasons to be grateful:

Ways to move my body:

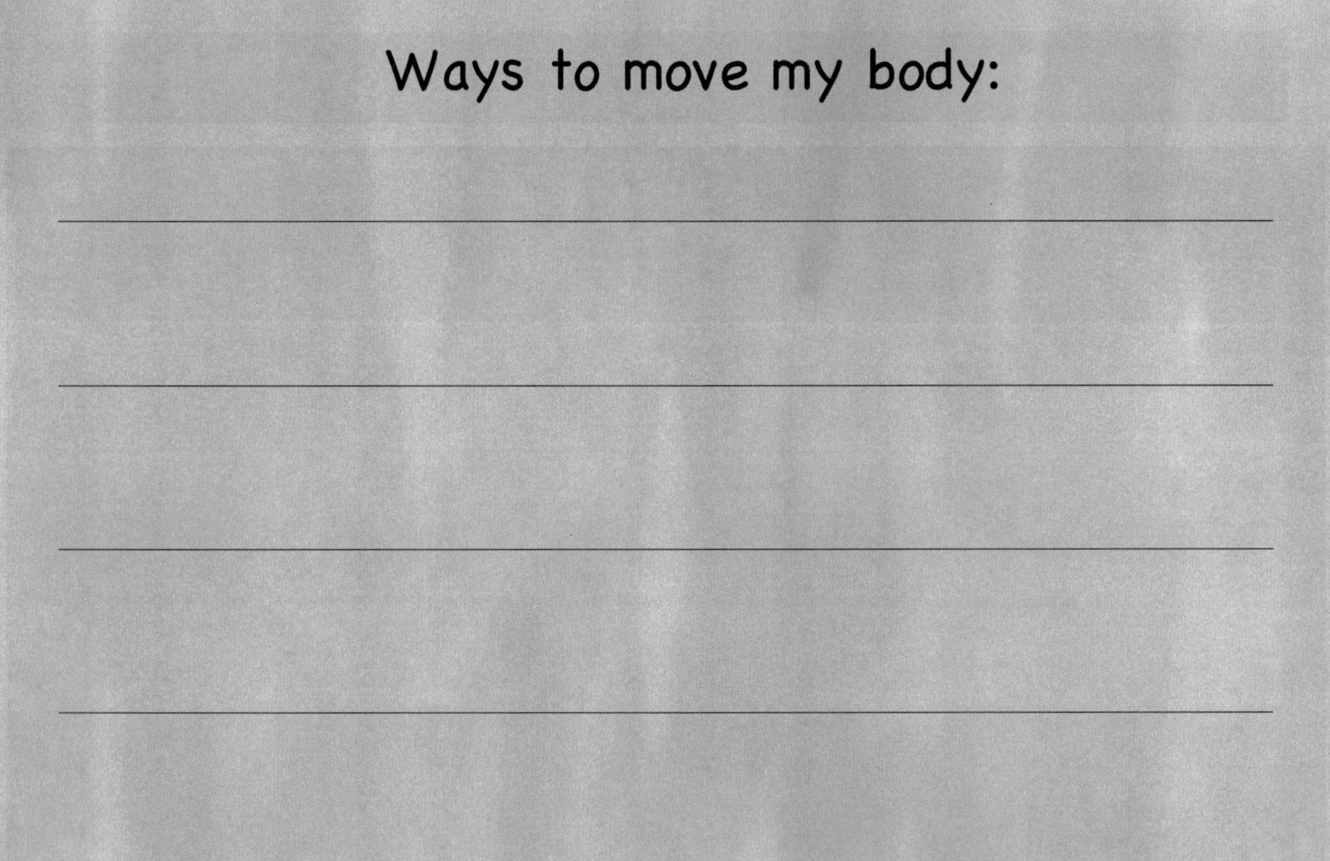

Made in the USA
Las Vegas, NV
17 November 2021